S0-ARG-305

For Lexi! :-♡ ♡ ♡ =:-

Isabella's Special Wish

By Deborah Belica

Illustrated by Elizabeth Karsch

Deborah Belica

Halo ●●●●
Publishing International

Isabella's Special Wish
Copyright© 2013 Deborah Designs
By Deborah Belica
Illustrated by Elizabeth Karsch
Layout & typography Susan Herbst
Garden City, New York
Website: www.isabellasspecialwish.com
E-mail: deborahbelica@gmail.com
All rights reserved.

No part of this book may be reproduced in any manner without
the written consent of the publisher except for brief excerpts
in critical reviews or articles.

ISBN 13: 978-1-61244-192-4
Library of Congress Control Number: 2013909456

Printed in the United States of America

Halo
Publishing International
www.halopublishing.com

Published by Halo Publishing International
AP·726
P.O. Box 60326
Houston, Texas 77205
Toll Free 1-877-705-9647
www.halopublishing.com
www.holapublishing.com
e-mail: contact@halopublishing.com

Dedicated to
Elizabeth,
Johnny, Georgia
and Nina

There once was a girl named Umbrella.

You can't name a girl Umbrella!

There once was a girl named Isabella.

She went to talk to a string.

You can't talk to a string!

She went to talk to a king.

She walked down a toad.

You can't walk down a toad!

She walked down a road.

She stopped to smell a tower.

You can't smell a tower!

She stopped to smell a flower.

She climbed up a bee.

You can't climb up a bee!

She climbed up a tree.

She walked up the chairs.

You can't walk up the chairs!

She walked up the stairs.

She asked the king for a tuna fish.

You can't ask the king for a tuna fish!

She asked the king for a special wish.

A special wish to keep inside a fox.

You can't keep a special wish inside a fox!

BOX
FOR
WISHES
!

A special wish to keep inside a box.

What was her special wish?

Was it a tuna fish?

Was it chairs or stairs?

Was it a bee or a tree?

Was it a tower or a flower?

Was it a toad or a road?

Was it a string, she asked of the king?

Was it an umbrella?

What was the special wish for Isabella?

She asked for a big box of bugs.

You can't ask a king for
a big box of bugs!

But you can ask for a big box of giggles and hugs!

That she can share with a cinnamon bun.

You can't share giggles and hugs
with a cinnamon bun!

But you can share giggles and hugs
with everyone!

Deborah Belica is a grandmother and dog lover who writes and paints from a seaside studio overlooking the Long Island Sound.

Elizabeth Karsch is an artist and mother on the East End of Long Island. She illustrates in the wee hours, after everyone else is tucked into bed.

Susan Herbst (layout & typography) is a mermaid who lives on the North Shore of Long Island.